For big sisters and little sisters

Katherine Tegen Books is an imprint of HarperCollins Publishers.

ISBN 978-0-06-291606-8

The artist used acrylic, gouache, colored pencil, crayon, and Photoshop to create the illustrations for this book. • Typography by Chelsea C. Donaldson

21 22 23 24 25 RTLO 10 9 8 7 6 5 4 3 2 1 ❖ First Edition

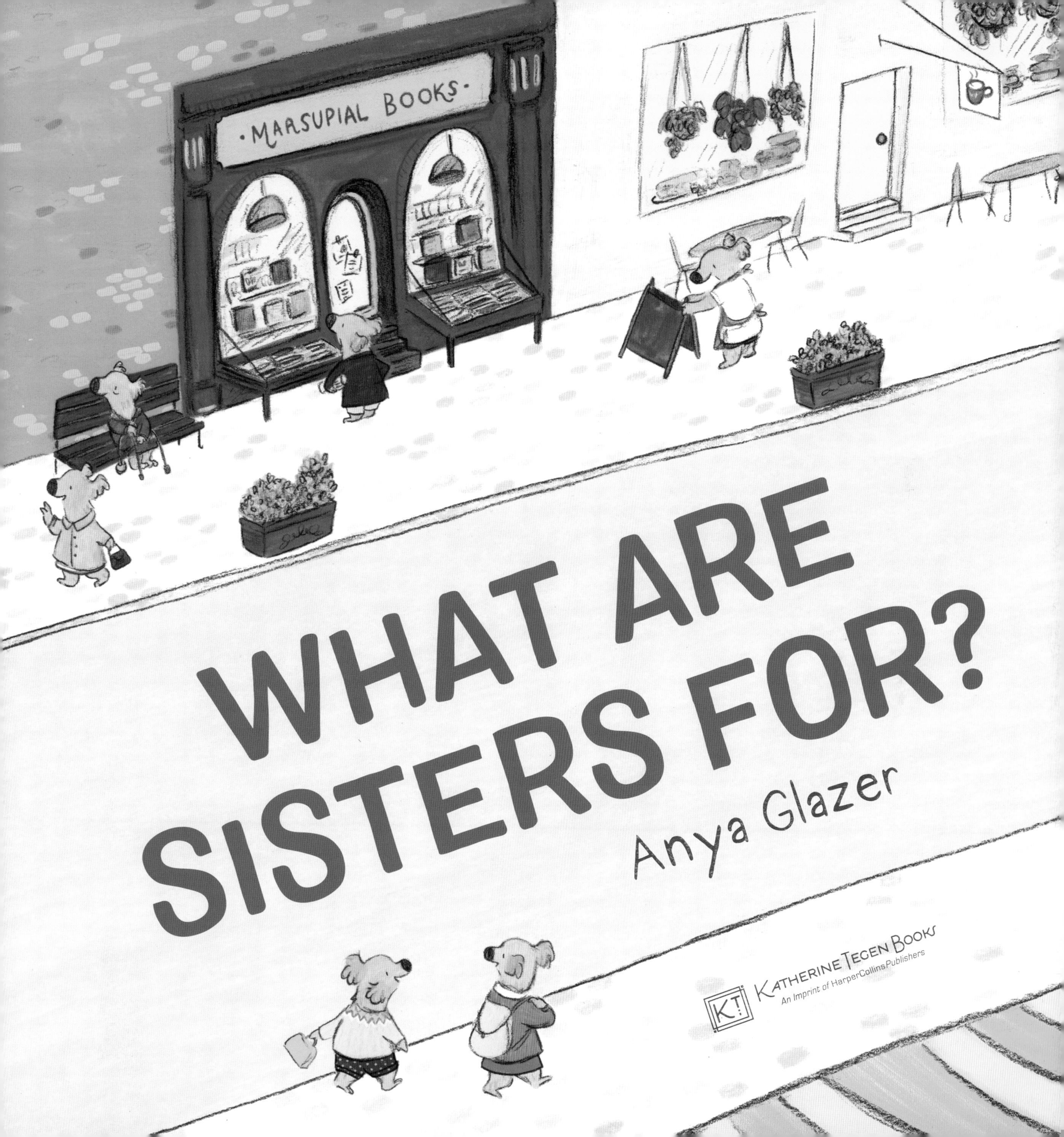

·MARSUPIAL BOOKS·
WHAT ARE SISTERS FOR?
Anya Glazer
KT
KATHERINE TEGEN BOOKS
An Imprint of HarperCollinsPublishers

FOODS
25

Bea's big sister, Ada, knew everything.

Which was good, because . . .

Bea had a lot of questions.

(Like I said, a LOT of questions.)

But Ada liked having all the answers—
that's what big sisters are for.

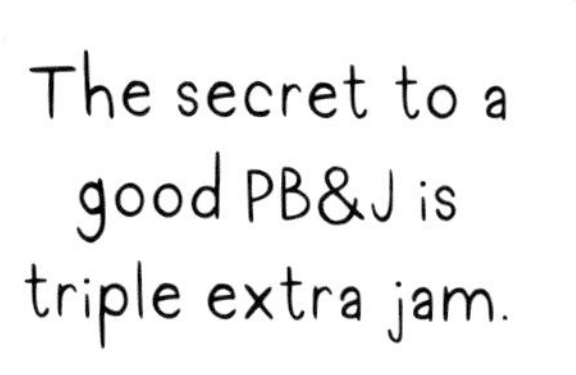

Lately, though, the questions were getting harder.
What happens when we sleep?

And Ada was struggling to keep up,

especially when the questions came late at night.

But big sisters ALWAYS have answers.

(Even when they don't.)

As Bea grew more curious, things were getting more complicated for Ada.

Hmm, I guess that would be somewhere in the jungle.
And what happens then?

They sprout from the ground as starberries.

No it's not. Tomorrow is Saturday! So can we go?

Ada knew she was (probably) wrong,
but she couldn't admit that to Bea.

So into the jungle they went.

What's the tallest tree?

Inside the jungle there were
a lot of things that Ada knew.

Trees can grow for thousands of years.
I think that's an armadillo . . . or maybe just a rock.
What's over there?

And even more that
Ada didn't know.

But Bea didn't mind.

She just carried on asking questions.

Do you think we're lost?
I think we might be lost.
You haven't seen any starberries yet, have you?

And finally Ada had had enough.
I DON'T KNOW!

I don't know where we are or where we're going.
And we probably won't find any starberries because I think I made them up.
And I don't really know what happens to shooting stars or if trees have feelings or how to speak fish,
even though big sisters are supposed to know EVERYTHING.
We should just go home.

But they couldn't go back, because they didn't know the way.

So Bea decided they should keep going forward instead.

And that's what they did.

What's that?
I don't know. . . .
What do you think?

Oh, Ada, LOOK!

There was, after all, still plenty to discover.

But it was time to go.

And somehow, the way
back was simple.
YAWN
Didn't we pass
that tree on the
way here?

And when they got home

and put their feet up

and made hot chocolate

and more peanut butter sandwiches
with triple extra jam,

it was Ada who had a
question for Bea . . .

Where shall we go next?

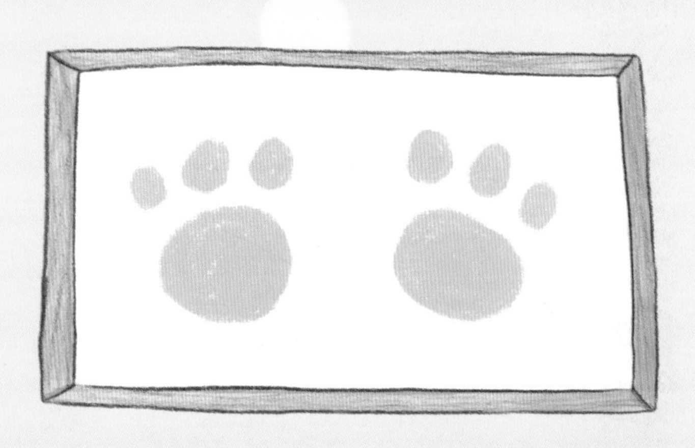